Reuben Aldridge Guild

Memorial address on the late John Whipple Potter Jenks

Professor of Zoology Emeritus and Curator of the Museums, Delivered

Before the Faculty and Students of Brown University in Sayles Memorial

Hall, February 6, 1895

Reuben Aldridge Guild

Memorial address on the late John Whipple Potter Jenks
*Professor of Zoology Emeritus and Curator of the Museums, Delivered Before the
Faculty and Students of Brown University in Sayles Memorial Hall, February 6, 1895*

ISBN/EAN: 9783337139582

Printed in Europe, USA, Canada, Australia, Japan

Cover: Foto ©Andreas Hilbeck / pixelio.de

More available books at **www.hansebooks.com**

MEMORIAL ADDRESS

ON THE LATE

John Whipple Potter Jenks, A.M.

PROFESSOR OF ZOOLOGY EMERITUS

AND

CURATOR OF THE MUSEUMS.

DELIVERED BEFORE THE

Faculty and Students of Brown University,

IN

SAYLES MEMORIAL HALL,

February 6, 1895.

BY

Reuben Aldridge Guild, A. M., LL. D.,

LIBRARIAN EMERITUS.

———————————

PROVIDENCE, R. I.:

PRESS OF CASEY BROTHERS, 7 COLLEGE ST.,

1895.

At a meeting of the Faculty of Brown University held shortly after Professor Jenks' lamented decease, suitable resolutions were adopted to be placed on their records, and a committee of three was appointed to secure a memorial address. The committee consisted of Alpheus S. Packard, M. D., Ph. D., Professor of Zoology and Geology, Herman C. Bumpus, Ph. D., Professor of Comparative Anatomy, and Assistant Curator of the Museums, and George W. Field, Ph. D., Associate Professor of Cellular Biology.

We have assembled this day to pay a tribute of gratitude and esteem to a departed associate;—one who lately trod these familiar walks, engaged in the daily routine of college life, and worshipped with us the Father of Lights and Mercies. To me it is allotted to commemorate his virtues in a brief sketch of his character and life. In the language of the revered Wayland on a similar occasion I may say, the great and the good with whom I have been officially connected for half a century have most of them passed away,—and now another link in the chain has been severed. I seem to myself the representative of a by-gone generation, and with mingled emotions address myself to the service which the partiality of your committee has imposed upon me.

For the first time in the history of the University, a beloved Professor has been stricken down at his post, dying upon the College premises. President Manning, indeed, was struck with apoplexy in the midst of the summer term, but he was in his house with his family around him. In these later years Professors Dunn, Diman, Greene, Bancroft and Lincoln have all had memorial services. Professor Dunn died at his father's house in Newport during the summer vacation. Professor Diman died in term time after a brief illness of six days, and Professor Greene was stricken down while on his way to College. Professor Lincoln, whom we all remember so well, died after a lingering sickness, on account of which he ceased from active instruction.

The subject of my sketch, John Whipple Potter Jenks, was a native of Massachusetts. He descended from a family not unknown to fame in the annals of Rhode Island. Joseph, his great ancestor, migrated from Buckinghamshire in England, and became the founder of Pawtucket. Each of his four sons was prominent in the history of the Colony. Joseph, the eldest, of "happy memory," was a leading member of the Baptist church in Providence, for several years Governor of the State, and at one time a representative at the Court of St. James. The second son became the military leader of all the forces in the Colony. The third son, Ebenezer, was an Elder in the church. His son Daniel, familiarly known as "Judge Jenckes," was a wealthy merchant of Providence, and a patron both of the College and the church. For many years he was a prominent member of the General Assembly, where he rendered essential service in the matter of the College Charter. His daughter Rhoda, it may be added, married a Brown, and thus became the mother of the noted benefactor who gave to the University its name. The fourth son, William, the direct ancestor of the Massachusetts branch of the family, became a Chief Justice, and died at the advanced age of ninety-one.

Professor Jenks was the sixth child and eldest son of Doct. Nicholas and Betsey (Potter) Jenks, and was born in West Boylston, on the first day of May,

1819. His mother was a daughter of Capt. John Potter, a man of great stature, a revolutionary soldier, and a Paymaster at Valley Forge. Often would he tell to his eager listening children and grandchildren, the story of the sufferings of the patriotic men who paraded on the frozen ground with bare and bleeding feet. His father, a native of North Brookfield, Massachusetts, was one of four sons, of whom Hervey was graduated at Brown University with the valedictory honors of his class. He himself was fitted for the medical profession, studying at the academies of Woodstock and Leicester, and afterwards with the celebrated Doct. John Green of Worcester. Upon the completion of his studies he commenced practice in West Boylston, teaching school during the winter months, as was the custom with professional men of limited incomes. During a revival of religion that swept over all that section of the country both father and mother were converted, embracing the sentiments of the Baptists. This they did upon a careful and independent study of the New Testament in reference to church polity, there being no Baptist church or preacher in the neighborhood. In consequence of this change in their religious views, the good Doctor lost his practice, the prevailing sentiments of the people around him being those of the "Standing Order." He was compelled, therefore, to seek a livelihood elsewhere.

About twenty-five miles distant in the southern part of the county bordering on Connecticut, was a small township that had been set off from Sturbridge, by the name of Southbridge. Thither the family removed when young Jenks was about a year old;—and here his childhood and early youth were spent. The religious community at Southbridge was about equally divided between Baptists and Congregationalists, who worshipped alternately in the one meeting-house of the place, which was also used as the town house. The Professor in his private memoirs gives a glowing description of this old fashioned, yellow painted, two story building, with low steeple and a bell. On three sides was a gallery, and on the fourth side a high pulpit that brought the minister's head above the level of the gallery floors. On the ceiling, back of the pulpit, was a fresco of two large owls' heads with big staring eyes, and wings dropping downward three feet, the whole designed to represent the angels overshadowing the Mercy Seat. Square pews that compelled a part of the occupants to sit with backs and sides to the minister, and seats that turned on hinges for convenience of standing, and, in the words of the Professor, "slammed with a bang at the close of the prayer," completed the interior. The use of cushions would have been deemed sacrilegious in those days, and foot stoves for the aged and infirm were the only means of warmth in winter.

Physically the elder brother of the family was somewhat precocious, as also mentally, being able to read, it is said, when a little more than three years old. At the age of five or six he was required to aid his sisters in making wool cards and braiding straw. Thus early were habits of industry and self-reliance instilled into his mind. Another of his employments was carrying a daily paper to the homes of the subscribers. From the age of four he was kept at school ten months in the year, and drilled at home in the elementary branches. As a result he was at thirteen beyond the ordinary text-books of the districts; and by attending a select school in the village he had gone through works on Natural Philosophy, Astronomy and Advanced History. He was furthermore a natural speller, and invariably "spelled down," in the phraseology of the day, all others in the school, although many of the scholars were his seniors. These details, trivial though they may appear, are important as illustrating his after career. The child is father of the man.

In the month of February preceding his eighth birthday, the monotony of his childhood life was broken somewhat by a sleigh ride to Providence, in company with his parents and a sister. They stopped for a time with Dr. Messer, who was a relative by marriage, his wife's mother being a Jenks*. He had recently resigned the Presidency of the University, and was now living in the "Messer House," so called, in the south western part of the town. Many times afterwards the lad recalled the stately mansion with its tall pillars and portico, spacious rooms and lofty ceilings, associating with it the glories of the Institution over which the owner had long presided, and with which he himself was to be so long and so

---

*The wife's maiden name was Deborah Angell.

honorably connected. The house has recently been taken down. This visit and a subsequent one to Amherst determined young Jenks upon a College life.

He was now approaching his thirteenth year, and it became necessary to make choice of some kind of business or a profession for the future. The father had already made arrangements with a watchmaker and jeweller to take him as an apprentice until he was eighteen, leaving it for the son to decide the matter on his coming birthday. The decision was promptly made. He would go to College. His father could only give his approval, and his time until he was twenty-one. The lad foresaw the struggle and self-denial involved in the task before him, but his energy and indomitable will, even at that early age, knew no obstacles. Making arrangements with a merchant farmer opposite his father's house to assist him in his work, go on errands and the like, for his board and clothing, he made a similar arrangement for his tuition with his pastor, the Rev. Addison Parker, and commenced the study of Latin. While reciting in the pastor's study from day to day, he attracted the notice of a young man visiting at the parsonage, who, on learning his history, offered to take the lad with him to Virginia, where he had been teaching for the past two years, pay all his expenses and fit him for College. The Maecenas* thus prov-

---

*In the Journal or Diary of Prof. Jenks occurs the following entry:— "Thursday, April 16, 1885. Called upon the Rev. Dr. Parker, the Maecenas who took me at the age of thirteen from Massachusetts to Virginia to attend his school, and begin to fit for College in the Classics. He at the age of seventy-nine had given up active service as a pastor, and was living in Los Angeles, with his married daughter."

identially found was the late Rev. Dr. Joseph W. Parker, a native of Vermont, and a recent graduate of Union College. This offer so generously made was gladly accepted, and he at once started on what was then a long journey, going by stage through Hartford, New York, Princeton, Philadelphia and Washington. His place of destination was the plantation of Nicholas Edmunds, in Charlotte County, Virginia, about ten miles from the Court House, and a mile from any residence. The school taught by Mr. Parker consisted of Mr. Edmunds' family, and as many more pupils as the little twenty-feet square log school house would accommodate. Here young Jenks continued the study of Latin and commenced Greek. Under the judicious and faithful guidance of his teacher, his religious convictions, which he had before leaving home as the result of a revival in the neighborhood, were deepened, until he was brought to a saving knowledge of the truth, and to an experience of the peace of God which passeth all understanding. At this point his religious life commenced, to be continued through all the changes and vicissitudes of subsequent years. Prayer now became his delight and the Bible his constant companion and guide.

During his sojourn in Virginia he was brought into contact with wild animal life, and he learned to use the gun, in the use of which he afterwards became an expert. His taste for Natural History was here developed. He saw nature in her varied aspects.

Squirrels, rabbits, opossums and reptiles abounded in the woods through which he daily passed, and fox hunting and boar hunting were pastimes in which, boy though he was, he not unfrequently engaged.

At the close of the year, his kind friend and bene-factor having decided to prosecute his studies at the Newton Theological Institution, he returned to his home in Southbridge, where, on the 9th of June, 1833, he was publicly baptised and received as a member of the church. During his absence a brother-in-law, the Rev. Hervey Fitts, had become pastor of the Baptist church in Middleboro, and now he offered his young relative a home while he should pursue his studies at the Pierce Academy. Here he remained another year and then entered Brown University, being the first one of his class to be matriculated. He was now in the beginning of his sixteenth year, small in stature but vigorous in health and strength, poor in purse, rich in hope, de-termined in purpose, and filled with a holy enthusi-asm to do the work to which he felt that he had been divinely called. Such was the lad who, on the second day of the term called on President Wayland to know what he could do to pay expenses. Looking kindly down upon him the good President gave him work in his garden, for which he paid him full wages. This was his first experience in college life, and it was full of promise. As winter set in and he could no longer do garden work, he obtained per-mission of the Steward to take charge of some recitation rooms, and also of the private rooms of several of the college officers. He sawed wood, carrying it from the cellar to the second, third and fourth stories. All work that was lawful was to him honorable. What he desired was to pay his own way and be independent. During his Junior and Senior years he taught in a Ladies' School, and in addition had lads in his room as private scholars. In going to and from college in vacations, a distance of forty miles, he usually walked, not being able to pay a stage coach fare.

There were at this time two tables in Commons Hall, at one of which board was ninety-five cents per week, and at the other one dollar and a quarter. Young Jenks commenced at the former table, but finding even this too expensive, he left and boarded himself, continuing to do this for two years, at an average cost of fifty cents per week. At one time while eating his frugal breakfast of brown bread and molasses, dried herring and cold water, a wealthy gentleman whom he had known in Middleboro, unexpectedly called at his room, and seeming surprised, asked him if that was his usual fare. The reply was that sometimes, when he had a fire he made hasty pudding, or boiled some rice. A five dollar bill which was sent him soon afterwards with a suggestion that he procure more wholesome food, was promptly returned with sincere and most grateful acknowledgments. The poor student was happy and contented; his present living met his wants;

his health was good, his appetite was excellent, and he did not wish to be beholden for favors which it was out of his power to return. We are reminded by this incident of the reply of the patriotic Marion, to the British officer whom he had invited to dine on roast potatoes. Is this, said the officer in astonishment, the fare of yourself and your men? Yes, said the imperturbable Marion, except that sometimes, when we can get it, we have a little salt.

It may be interesting to know what was the daily college routine of this period. The first bell was rung at half past five. Prayers were held in the old chapel at a quarter before six, which for a part of the year would be at candle light. Recitations until seven followed prayers, after which came breakfast in Commons Hall, and then recreation until nine when study hours commenced. The second hour for recitations was eleven, followed by dinner at twelve, and recreation until two, when study hours again commenced. The third recitation hour was from four until five, when all assembled in the chapel once more for prayers, after which came a declamation from a Junior, or an original piece from a Senior, spoken from the stage in front of the Faculty. Supper followed, and then recreation until seven. Study hours in the evening were from seven until nine, when all were expected to retire. A division of each dormitory was assigned to a member of the Faculty, whose duty it was to make from one to three visits a day in study hours to see if all were in their rooms. Such was college life in the days of Professor Jenks. During his entire course of four years he never had, as he himself states, a tardy mark, nor did he lose a day's recitation on account of sickness or absence. He attended all the meetings of the Philermenian Debating Society of which he was a member, the prayer meetings of his class on Friday evenings, the meetings of the Religious Society on Wednesday evenings, and the monthly meetings of the Society for Missionary Inquiry. His example as a Christian man is in this respect worthy of imitation. During a part of his course he conducted a Bible class in Olneyville, and during his Senior year he was Superintendent of the Third Baptist, now the Union Baptist Sunday School. He was strict in his attendance upon Dr. Wayland's Bible class, which was held each Sunday afternoon after the preaching service. The Dr. was accustomed to use the Greek text, arranging to go through the New Testament every four years. When he reached Revelation, says Jenks, he would say: "Young gentlemen we will begin the New Testament again, as I do not understand Revelation, but hope to some time, probably not in this life."

When he entered college his class numbered according to the catalogue, forty-three, and he found himself standing in scholarship forty-one, or nearly at the foot. He had not the grammatical knowledge of Latin and Greek which others of his class possessed, who had fitted at the schools of Boston and

Providence, and at the renowned academies of Andover and Exeter. He was about the youngest in age, and in purse certainly the poorest. The class numbered at graduation thirty, and his rank was nine, having assigned him for his part at Commencement, a conference with Edward D. Pearce and Alexander Burgess. This is the class, be it remembered, which Professor Gammell was accustomed to characterize as the ablest in the point of talent and influence of which he had personal knowledge. Among its members was Robinson, late the honored President of the University; Bradley, the Valedictorian, Chief Justice of the Supreme Court of Rhode Island; Ames, the Salutatorian, who died soon after graduation; Morton, Chief Justice of the Supreme Court of Massachusetts; Burgess, Bishop of Illinois; Lothrop, Envoy Extraordinary and Minister Plenipotentiary to the Court of Russia; Wilson, Judge of the Circuit Court of Illinois, and the leading lawyer in that State; Thomas A. Jenckes, one of the ablest Representatives to Congress from this or any State, the author of Civil Service Reform; Cole, President of a Theological Institution; Clarke, for nine years City Solicitor of Providence; and Arnold, Bowers, Dike, Reed, Stockbridge, Sumner and Tustin, all Doctors of Divinity. To have attained the rank of nine in such a class, under adverse circumstances, indicates perseverance, and talent of no ordinary character.

At length the last term of the Senior year drew to a close, and he was led to recall the words of his mother in his Freshman year: "John, by being faithful to your daily work as assigned you by the Faculty, and by daily consecration of yourself as a Christian, make the most of your college course, for it ought to be the happiest period of your life. Your daily work is planned by others, and you have only to do your duty without care or anxiety. But after graduation you will have to plan for yourself as well as execute, and coming into contact with unreasonable people, you will find life very different from your present experience." Wise counsel this, showing the home influences to which he had been subjected in childhood, and giving a key to his character and usefulness as afterwards developed. He had indeed been faithful in the performance of every allotted task, and he had daily sought the guidance and blessing of Him to whom he had consecrated his life. He had spent for his education just nine hundred dollars, of which he had earned two thirds by manual labor and teaching, borrowing from the Education Society the remaining three hundred. With this exception he had fulfilled the Apostle's injunction, "Owe no man anything." While he was planning for the future, President Wayland received a letter from one Judge Warren, residing in a small village in Southern Georgia, requesting him to send them immediately a teacher who was both a graduate and a Christian. Knowing that Abolitionism was an agitating subject in the land, the offer was made to Jenks, who had spent a year in Virginia, and was presumed to be more or less familiar with slavery. Getting excused from the exercises of Commencement, which occurred in September, and procuring a suitable outfit, he set out for the South, arriving at his place of destination in August. Americus, which was the name of the village, was then a small hamlet in the forest, consisting of about a dozen families, who two years before had emigrated from the Carolinas, and settled upon Government land which had belonged to the Lower Creek Indians. There were about forty families in the neighborhood, and like other frontier communities, they exhibited a civilization but little removed from that of the Aborigines. With but few exceptions they were poor and wretched. Horse racing, drinking, swearing, cursing and ignorance everywhere abounded. In the young graduate they found indeed what they so much needed, a Christian teacher. Devoting all his energies to the work before him he soon won respect, and secured from the better class hearty co-operation. Here he remained eighteen months, teaching in a little log school house, preaching in the Court house so called, attending funerals, visiting the sick, and in various ways elevating the tone of society and infusing into it the principles and restraints of Christianity. The little hamlet has now become a flourishing city, and near the spot where he ministered to an infant, struggling church is now a fine brick meeting house, which it was his privilege in later years (1890) to assist in dedicating.

During the latter part of his stay in Americus, there was a powerful revival of religion which extended throughout the neighborhood far and wide. Some of his older pupils and many of his hearers were converted. One of the most prominent converts was a man of powerful frame and wicked life, who for months had dogged his path with a loaded gun, intending to shoot him down for correcting a young nephew in the school room. Indeed, he had once seized his horse by the bridle while crossing a creek, and struck him a violent blow. Now he became the teacher's warmest friend.

In the beginning of the year 1840, he resigned his position at Americus, to accept a call to become the colleague of Dr. Mercer, the popular and beloved pastor of the Baptist Church in Washington, Wilkes County. This at the time was perhaps the wealthiest and most aristocratic inland town of Georgia, having three churches, a bank, a fine Female Seminary, and Mercer University not far away. Here the *Index*, still the organ of the denomination in the State, was published. Dr. Mercer, who was now advanced in years and in feeble health, was regarded as the most noted preacher of his faith in all the South. He was for several years editor of the *Index*, which he had purchased of Dr. Brantly and transferred from Philadelphia, and he was the founder of the University which bears his name. Among his hearers were many wealthy planters, including Robert Tombs, afterwards the famous secessionist, and Alexander H. Stevens, the noted Vice President of the Southern Confederacy. Here Mr. Jenks labored with success eleven months, occupying the pulpit Sunday mornings, conducting the prayer and conference meetings, visiting the sick, and aiding in the publication of the weekly paper. As he was intending at this time to devote his life to missionary service in China he studied medicine with Doct. Ficklen a noted physician of the place, whose daughter, it may be added, was afterwards married to Dr. Boyce, a graduate of Brown, and the founder of the Theological Seminary at Louisville.

Dr. Mercer was now rapidly approaching his end, and the church accordingly extended a formal and unanimous invitation to Mr. Jenks to be ordained and become their settled pastor. This invitation, so flattering to a young man not yet twenty-one, and so indicative of the high estimation in which his pulpit talents and resources were regarded by an intelligent community, he felt compelled to decline, not having had a theological training. An invitation to become co-principal of the Female Seminary, and also an adjunct professor in Mercer University he also declined, preferring to take charge for ten months of a planter's school in Taliafere County. He returned home in the early part of the year 1842, having labored in the South three years and four months.

Peirce Academy, with which Mr. Jenks was henceforth to be so prominently identified, and where the prime of his life was spent, had been founded as early as the year 1808, by Deacon Levi Peirce, for the twofold purpose of securing a hall for public worship and rooms for a school. Like many other institutions of a similiar character, the first few years of its existence were years of struggle and varied fortunes. In 1828, a house of worship having been built by Deacon Peirce on the lot adjoining the Academy, both the house and the academy building, with the lots on which they stood, were deeded to the Central Baptist Society. Subsequently the Academy passed into the hands of trustees, an act of incorporation having been obtained from the State Legislature in 1835. The School was now in a languishing condition, indeed, was almost defunct, so that its revival to an ordinary mind seemed an herculean if not a hopeless task. The number of its pupils had dwindled down to fifteen, the building was old and dilapidated, there were no funds, and there was no apparatus, not even a blackboard upon the walls. Under these discouraging circumstances the position of Principal was offered to Mr. Jenks, with the understanding that he was to take the School into his own hands, run it upon its merits, and pay all expenses. Here was the great opportunity of his life. He saw all the difficulties before him, but he was not dismayed. He had been accustomed from boyhood to habits of self-reliance. He had resistless energy, a courage that knew no danger, and a boundless faith in the Supreme Ruler and Disposer, to whom he had committed all his ways. Rejecting flattering offers of other positions he accepted this one, mainly, as he himself states, because this was a private institution, founded under the auspices of a denomination to which he was warmly attached, and where he could cultivate without let or hindrance the religious sentiments, as well as train the intellect. It is no disparagement perhaps to add, that Middleboro was the home of one whom he had loved from boyhood, and to whom on attaining to manhood he had plighted his troth.

On the first Monday in March, 1842, he commenced the term with eleven pupils, closing with thirty. The second term he commenced with sixty pupils and closed with eighty. His success was now assured, and he entered into matrimonial relations, making it his permanent home with his father-in-law, the late Major Elisha Tucker. His wife was an only child, the granddaughter of the founder of the Academy, and a lady of rare personal attractions and moral worth. For nearly forty-two years they walked in happy union such as is seldom accorded to mortals in this present life, until in July, 1884, the golden cord was severed. During all this period of complete domestic bliss, their hopes, their joys, their interests, their fortunes were one, and not a jarring word of discord ever passed their lips.

Having by strict economy succeeded in obtaining a valuable apparatus, and having a School of one hundred pupils with a constantly increasing attendance, Mr. Jenks now began to indulge his passion for the study of nature, particularly in Ornithology, taking lessons of a celebrated taxidermist in Boston for the purpose of making a collection. In this his enthusiasm knew no bounds. It became no uncommon thing for him to rise before daylight and spend two hours with his gun, mounting his birds from nine until midnight. In this manner, and by purchase and exchange, he in the course of ten years secured a Museum superior to that of any academy in New England, and which attracted the attention of men of science. It had cost him an outlay of thousands of dollars, besides an infinite amount of time and labor. Eventually he presented it to the Academy. Upon the closing up of the Academy in the year 1879, the trustees presented it to the South Jersey Institute in Bridgeton, where it is now known and designated as the " Peirce Collection."

At the second meeting of the American Association for the Advancement of Science, Mr. Jenks became a member, signing the constitution at the same time with his beloved teacher in College, Dr. Caswell. The annual meetings of this Association he attended with greater or less regularity up to the last year of his life. I cannot learn from the published proceedings that he was prominent on committees, or that he often read papers. He was too busy a man by far to make original investigations. His life work as a scientist was that of a collector, and this work he loved. His connection with this Association brought him into pleasant relations with distinguished men, with some of whom, especially Professor Baird of the Smithsonian Institution, and Professor Agassiz, who was not unfrequently his honored guest at Middleboro, he formed intimacies which only death interrupted. To the latter he rendered important service in the preparation of his great work on the Embryology of the Turtle; a service which the author gratefully acknowledges in his preface. About this time he was appointed Professor of Zoology in the Massachusetts Horticultural Society, a position of honor without salary, the duties being merely of consultation. The meetings were held fortnightly in Boston. On one occasion a member, who was at the same time State Senator, presented a petition in favor of rescinding the law that protected the Robin, saying he had found it very destructive to fruits. Through Mr. Jenks' influence the petition was laid upon the table, he promising to ascertain the food of the bird for every month of the year. This he did in a most satisfactory manner, showing that the Robin was far more beneficial by destroying worms and insects during ten months in the year, than destructive by eating garden fruits in July and August. The report was published in the proceedings of the Society, and has often been quoted as an authority upon the subject of which it treats.

Time will not allow me to enter further into the details of his career in Middleboro. During the twenty-nine years of his administration as Principal of the Academy, it attained to a very high rank, having at one time a roll call of three hundred pupils of both sexes, averaging over eighteen years of age. Among his corps of assistants were the noted teachers, Charles C. Burnett, and John M. Manning, both graduates of Brown. A new building was erected and again and again enlarged, partly at the Principal's expense. Distinguished divines were invited to address the Society for Missionary Inquiry, and distinguished orators and poets the Literary Debating Society. Crowds of alumni and friends attended the annual graduating exercises similar to a college commencement, making the town joyous as on a festive occasion. In 1858 occurred the semi-centennial of the Academy, and it was made a Jubilee Celebration, Hon. Benjamin F. Hallet, an alumnus, giving the oration, George C. Burgess the poem, and Mr. Jenks the historical address. The year following he spent five months in travel abroad, visiting the principal cities and places of interest, and delighting in the great Cabinets and Museums, to which a letter of introduction from Professor Agassiz proved an open sesame. During the Civil War many of his pupils enlisted, and the School, like all other institutions of learning, felt the depressing effects of domestic strife. Afterwards high schools and normal schools, established and maintained at the expense of the State, took the place of academies, and private schools one after another ceased to exist. Notwithstanding all this Peirce Academy continued to flourish until the year 1871, when the Principal, having completed his allotted term of thirty-three years, or a generation from the time of his graduation from College, and in accordance with a determination previously expressed, handed in his resignation to the Board of Trustees. In taking leave of him in this connection, an incident which I find recorded in his journal may be of interest, illustrating as it does the widespread reputation and influence of the man.*

Soon after the war, a fine looking gentleman in middle life called at the Academy door, and remarked that being on the way from Boston to New Bedford, he thought he would stop long enough to visit Peirce Academy, of the fame of which he had heard at various times. Inviting him to a seat on the platform, the Principal called up the first class, which was in French. The stranger requested that he might take a seat with the class and recite. Humoring this singular whim, his request was granted, and he was called upon in turn to translate, which he did very creditably. The next class was in Algebra, and keeping his seat the stranger desired to try his hand at that. In this also he succeeded, working out a problem on the blackboard. Till

*The Hon. John S. Brayton, LL. D., a graduate of Brown University, in the class of 1851, thus writes respecting his early instructor:

"I attended Pierce Academy in 1845, and have maintained the acquaintance which I then formed with Professor Jenks up to his death. He was a warm friend of mine. Mr. Jenks led a most active life; he was a great worker; enthusiastic in everything in which he became interested; was never tired in doing good, and always ready to aid and assist those who were deserving and needy. I regret that the Corporation of the University did not, during his life time, bestow upon him an honorary degree of Doctor of Laws, which he justly merited."

noon he kept his seat, with the several classes, and was called upon in turn to recite. At the close of the School he explained. My brother, he remarked, some years ago was a pupil here, and fitted for the Academy at West Point, where he was graduated. He was afterwards appointed one of the Professors, continuing at the Institution until he died. Of you he always spoke as laying the foundation of his success in life. I am a surgeon in the Navy, and for years have been sailing around the world, stopping for weeks now in one port, now in another. Our Commandants, while we are thus detained, are in the habit of inviting the officers of our merchant marine who may happen to be in port to a banquet on board the man of war. On such occasions the captains and mates are introduced to each other, and naturally inquire for each others homes. One would reply, "I am from Cape Cod." And another, "And so am I." Well, "were you ever in Middleboro"? "Yes, I went to school at Peirce Academy." "And so did I." "And do tell me if Professor Jenks is still Principal." "Yes, and as bright and active and good as ever." Such conversations I have listened to in every foreign port where my vessel has been detained. For my part I could only say, I had a brother taught by Professor Jenks, and only regretted that I had not had that same privilege. Now I can say I have been a pupil at Peirce Academy, and have recited to Professor Jenks. (Whether the stranger received a certificate of his proficiency in French and Algebra is not stated.)

The time seemed now to have arrived for him to carry into execution a purpose which he had long formed, of collecting for Brown University a Museum of Natural History. Professor Agassiz had once remarked in his presence that there were more investigators than collectors. The thought was to him an inspiration, and from that moment he determined to spend the closing years of his life in thus advancing the cause of science and religion. On the same day when he sent in his resignation as Principal, he addressed a formal communication to his friend and former instructor, Professor Caswell, now President of the University, offering his services. " For while," he said, " the College is one of the oldest institutions in the country, there is no one half as old that has not better facilities for illustrating any branch of Natural Science, and I am positively ashamed of my Alma Mater." The return mail brought a reply saying, " Come and dine with me on Saturday and we will talk Natural History." In conversation the President was found to be keenly alive to the existing deficiencies of the College, but said, " There is not a dollar in the treasury that can be devoted to the building up of a Museum." "And there never will be," was the reply, "until a beginning is made." The result was a beginning. Contributions to the amount of a thousand dollars were at once secured from friends of the enterprise. Two floor cases for minerals, fossils and shells, and an upright wall case for mounted birds were placed in Rhode Island Hall, and in three months time they were filled and arranged by Professor Jenks in readiness for the Commencement in June.

A pleasing incident may be mentioned in this connection. The Rev. Frederic Denison, a loyal alumnus of Brown, had been for many years making a collection of Indian relics in Connecticut and Rhode Island, and was now preparing an account of them for a history of Westerly, where he was settled as pastor of a church. A paragraph in the Providence *Journal* referring to this collection caught the eye of Professor Jenks, and soon he had an account of it from the author himself. Before there was time for a reply the Professor was in the pastor's study, his face all radiant with joy as he gazed upon the six hundred relics illustrating the history, manners and customs of the aborigines. The owner could have sold them for a handsome sum, but he gladly gave them as a foundation for the new Museum, and they were at once transferred to the cases in Rhode Island Hall. The next day a collector from Yale appeared on the ground, but he was twenty-four hours too late. The relics had gone. To this collection Mr. Denison and others have made additions, until it now numbers upwards of a thousand specimens, constituting a most interesting and valuable part of the Anthropological department.

At the meeting of the alumni in June following, the Professor made known his plans and purposes in regard to the Museum, and solicited the hearty co-operation of all graduates and friends of the College. He stated that during the past ten weeks he had obtained and mounted as a beginning, three hundred and forty-three specimens of birds, fifty birds' nests with eggs fresh from the forest and field, twenty reptiles, and quite a miscellaneous collection, including Indian relics, and a few specimens of minerals and shells that he had found stored away in the basement. His remarks were received with applause. President Caswell in his opening speech at the Commencement dinner invited the guests before leaving the grounds to visit the Hall, and see the beginning that had been made in what he hoped might prove an important means of culture. In his annual report to the Corporation he referred to the subject again, and spoke of the valuable labors of Professor Jenks, whom he designated as a "well informed naturalist and a most skillful taxidermist."

But though a favorable beginning had thus been made, the Corporation was not yet prepared to appropriate a dollar towards the continuance of the work, much less to appoint a permanent Curator with a salary. A special arrangement was therefore made with President Caswell, he guaranteeing to furnish funds through private subscriptions. In this he happily succeeded, securing during the year upwards of six thousand dollars. The enterprise was now fairly inaugurated. About this time the United States Fish Commission received its first appropriation from Congress, Professor Baird being the Commissioner and

Woods Holl the place of operations. As Professor Jenks was a warm personal friend of Baird, he was naturally solicited to become his assistant. This of course he could not now do. He, however, consented to attach himself to the Commission as a supernumerary, working as he had opportunity without pay, and being allowed the duplicates for Brown. This was a fortunate circumstance, as it gave him a prestige at the outset, and a valuable collection of Marine Fauna. Another fortunate circumstance: John Cassin, a noted Ornithologist and author, having just died, his collection, in skin and properly labelled, was on sale in Philadelphia. The Professor saw the advertisement, and without waiting to write, with his accustomed promptness, took the next train for the City of Brotherly Love. The price was three hundred dollars, and the number of skins was twenty-five hundred more or less. The money was at once paid, and the collection, numbering on count upwards of four thousand, was expressed to Providence. The next day a letter was received from Professor Agassiz wanting it for Harvard. He also, like the Yale collector, was twenty-four hours too late. The famous Blanding collection, to which Dr. Carpenter of Pawtucket had made allusion at the Alumni meeting in June, was through the perseverance and zeal of the new Curator, transferred from its temporary quarters at the homestead in Rehoboth to Rhode Island Hall. The founder of this collection, Dr. William Blanding, was a native of Rehoboth, and a graduate of Brown in the class of 1801. Having accumulated a competency in the practice of his profession, he had devoted the closing years of his life to his favorite study of Natural History, and to the gathering from every quarter of the globe of minerals, shells, fossils, birds, quadrupeds, reptiles, coins, medals and relics, making a collection believed at one time to be the largest of any private collection in the United States. He died in Rehoboth where he was born, leaving his treasures to distant relatives, who were only too glad to place them in the keeping of Professor Jenks.

But now the Corporation was in trouble in regard to the Agricultural Fund, so-called, the income of which had thus far been appropriated towards paying the tuition of beneficiaries designated by the State Legislature, without any special provision on the part of the College for instruction in Agriculture and the Mechanic Arts. An Investigating Committee had been appointed by Congress to inquire into the use each State was making of the funds created by the sale of the Agricultural Lands. This Committee required that the Corporation create a Professorship of Agriculture, and give special instruction to the beneficiaries, otherwise the State would be impeached and a demand made for a return of the Fund. In this emergency the Curator was earnestly requested to add to his duties the work of a Professor of Agriculture, his familiarity with domestic animals, and his experience in farming admirably qualifying him for the difficult and important position. An outline of twenty lectures hastily prepared, showing what he could do in this line, was read before the Joint Committees of the Legislature and the College. All parties were satisfied, and at the annual meeting of the Corporation, in June, 1872, he was formally appointed Director of the Museum of Natural History, and Lecturer on Special Branches of Agriculture. Subsequently his title was changed to Professor of Agricultural Zoology, and Curator of the Museum of Natural History. This title he retained until the day of his death, giving lectures as proposed, attending the meetings of the Faculty, and sustaining with increasing credit the important department of instruction committed to his charge. In his final report to President Andrews, published since his decease, he says: "For the twentieth time as Professor of Agricultural Zoology, I have delivered my annual course of lectures on Agricultural topics, each year revised and improved, to the members of the Senior Class enjoying the benefit of the State Agricultural Scholarships, and have only words of commendation as to both the deportment of the students, and the interest manifested in the subjects treated."

It would be interesting did time allow, to trace from these feeble beginnings the steady and continuous growth of our present Museum of Anthropology, and the Jenks Museum of Zoology. Through the personal solicitations of the zealous and indefatigable

Curator, and by means of circulars and letters, contributions from alumni and friends have been received almost daily during all the twenty-three years of his administration. The Zoological Gardens of New York, the Smithsonian Institution at Washington, the Fish Commission at Woods Holl, and the Museums of Harvard, Boston, and elsewhere, have all been laid under contribution for their duplicate treasures. Many of the finest and rarest specimens of Ornithology he himself shot in the wilds of Florida. They are all mentioned in detail in his annual reports to the President of the University. In 1871 he states that the collection in Rhode Island Hall numbered some fifteen hundred specimens; in 1872, eight thousand; in 1873, twenty-five thousand; in 1874, thirty-four thousand; in 1877, thirty-nine thousand; in 1878, forty-nine thousand. These figures give only an approximate idea of its growth. Some of the contributions have come from remote quarters of the globe. Thus we find mentioned in his reports, specimens of the various woods of Burma, neatly prepared and labelled, from the Rev. Dr. J. N. Cushing; specimens of Serpula, Pectens and Pottery, from the Rev. A. A. Bennett, of Japan; and a unique and valuable gift from the lamented Hartsock illustrating the manners and customs of the natives in the interior of Africa. From Horace F. Carpenter of Providence, came a complete set of the shells of Rhode Island, land, fresh water and marine; from Professor W. W. Bailey an Herbarium, and specimens in Botany beautifully mounted; from the Smithsonian Institution a complete set of North American Herpetology. The class of 1878 contributed a fine skin of a walrus, weighing in its natural state fully three thousand pounds. This the Professor stuffed at his home in Middleboro. The Rev. Dr. E. R. Beadle, a Presbyterian clergyman of Philadelphia now deceased, gave most valuable fossils, and various gifts from year to year, including a Royal Japanese Palanquin of most exquisite gilt and lacquer finish, richly embellished with the State seal and the Emperor's coat of arms. The late Zachariah Allen contributed a genuine suit of ancient metallic armor, with its accompaniment of sword and halberd, cross bow and fire lock, dating back to the year 1500. The family of Mr. Allen also contributed a fine collection of shells with cabinet case. From Professor Packard came instruments of stone and bronze illustrating Prehistoric Anthropology in Europe. These have all been arranged and labelled by the Curator, and most of the specimens in Zoology have been mounted, stuffed and otherwise prepared by his own skillful hands.

In the Winter and Spring of 1874, Professor Jenks spent five months hunting in the miasmatic swamps and everglades around Lake Okechobee in Southern Florida, a detailed account of which he afterwards published. As a result of this tour he collected at his own expense, and presented to the Museum, one hundred rare birds, two hundred rare eggs, a miscellaneous variety of fishes, reptiles, animals, insects, and relics of the Seminole Indians. The year 1885, following the lamented death of his wife, he spent in travel, visiting every state and territory in the Union, including Alaska, and also the Sandwich Islands, Mexico, British Columbia, Manitoba and Canada. Wherever he went he made collections of specimens for the Museum, and arranged with dealers for future correspondence. From this time on until the close of life his winters were spent in Florida, at a place which he termed Oak Lodge, on the Eastern coast.

Suffer me a few words more. In the year 1874 an addition was made to Rhode Island Hall, giving a separate room for the portraits, and enabling the Curator to complete the wall cases. Eventually the portraits were transferred to Sayles Memorial Hall, the botanical specimens were given over to the care of Professor Bailey, a department of Botany having been established in the College, and the new or East Room was devoted exclusively to Anthropology. At the annual meeting of the Corporation, in September, 1891, the main or west room was designated as the Jenks Museum of Zoology, to be recognized as such in the catalogues, and in the future history of the University. This was done in view not only of the persevering and self-sacrificing efforts of the founder, but also of his donations made from the savings of a small salary, and amounting at that time, according to his own statement, to upwards of six thousand dollars,

Professor Jenks now commenced in earnest the work of fitting up at his own expense, the new or East room for the rapidly accumulating stores of Anthropological material. He employed a foreman and four carpenters, constructed a large arch way connecting the two rooms, made a skylight, and upwards of thirty glass cases. This he did in addition to his previous donations. In his report for 1892, he says: "This additional room makes it possible for me to begin to realize what college museums of Zoology and Anthropology should be; and I trust it may please the All-wise Disposer of all earthly events to spare my life till my ideal shall have an approximate completion;—for as God's works of creation are infinite in variety and utility, so there can never be more than an approximation to that variety in any one museum collection." In his final report to President Andrews, published since his decease, he says:—"There is urgent need of another room for the Mineralogical and Geological cabinets, both that they may have the display worthy of their merit, and that the space they now anomalously occupy in the Museum of Zoology, may be utilized more legitimately, according to plans I have in mind, for constructing at my own expense, extension cases for specialties not yet attached to the Museum."

These cases he never lived to construct. His work was finished. On Wednesday, September 26th, he appeared in good health, attended to his duties, and went to his dinner as usual. Returning he was seized with heart failure, and fell prostrate at the foot of the stairs leading to the Museum, and there he was found by some visitors. He had always desired a sudden death, and his wish was granted. He was able to work to the last; he was spared the pangs of disease, and the anxieties of a prolonged sickness. " He was not for God took him."

The name of Professor Jenks seldom appears in the catalogues of authors. About year 1876 he was persuaded to prepare, as a part of Steele's fourteen weeks series of text books in the natural sciences, " Fourteen Weeks in Zoology." Having as he says, a natural distaste from childhood for appearing before the public in the role of an author, he refused to allow his name to appear on the title page. The book, which was published the year following, proved, unexpectedly to him, a great success, and a new edition was called for. In 1886 accordingly he both revised and rewrote the book, making it altogether a new work. In this second edition his name appears as the author, Professor Steele having died before its publication. So acceptable was the new edition, which is entitled " Popular Zoology," that the Chatauqua Assembly adopted it for their course in 1889, taking thirty thousand copies. Had the author's tastes so inclined, and his modesty not prevented, his name might have been handed down as a popular and instructive writer in Natural History. A third edition of his Zoology, with an addition on Practical Laboratory Teachings, by Dr. George W.

Field, Associate Professor of Cellular Biology, is now ready, I understand, for the press.

Professor Jenks possessed a remarkably cheerful temperament, and a disposition so genial, that he was always ready to do a friendly act, and never ready to speak an unkind or ill word. Hence he made friends wherever he went. He saw the types of Southern feeling as developed in slavery, secession, and reconstruction, and through it all preserved the most cordial relations with his early associates in Virginia and Georgia, as his journals and letters amply testify. He was withal a popular and instructive lecturer, and his services as such were in request by schools, academies and societies. While some are respected for their position, and esteemed for their abilities, he was respected, esteemed and *beloved* by his associates in the Faculty, his pupils at the Academy and College, and by all with whom he came in contact.

It may be interesting to know the views of Professor Jenks as a naturalist, on the Darwin theory of development, in relation to the origin of the human race. He believed with the inspired Apostle, that "God hath made of one blood" all the nations of the earth; that man was the completed work of Creation; that he was made in the image of God, a little lower than the angels, and crowned with glory and honor; that he was made to have dominion over the works of the Creator's hands; that in the words of the Psalmist, "all things were put under his feet, all sheep and oxen, yea, the beasts of the field, the fowl of the air, the fish of the sea, and whatsoever passeth through the paths of the seas." Monkeys and apes were not, in his opinion, thus created; and they formed no part of his anthropological collections.

While he saw the power and goodness of God displayed in the outward works of Creation, in the heavens the work of His fingers, and the moon and the stars which He had ordained, he also saw with equal clearness the same power and goodness displayed in God's Most Holy Word, revealed to man through inspired prophets, evangelists, and apostles. This he regarded as the great *Moral* Creation, and he received it with reverence and unfaltering trust, taking it from Genesis to Revelation as the man of his counsel and the guide of his life. At the last meeting of the American Association for the Advancement of Science, held in Brooklyn only five weeks before his decease, he was present, and took a prominent part in a prayer and conference meeting held Sunday afternoon by some sixty of the members. Remarking that he was the oldest member present, having attended the meetings of the Association from the beginning, he gave this testimony, as reported in the columns of the New York *World*: " In all his travels," he remarked, " in the wilds, in the jungle, and on the sea, he had always found a church in his Bible. If Science had sometimes travelled from the Bible truths, he had not. It was the INSPIRED WORD, and he had been led on by that

WORD in happiness and joy. Hold on to this Book," he said, " Consult it every day, and the love and goodness of the Lord will be manifest to you." In conclusion he urged the younger members not to give heed to the efforts of those who would disrupt the INSPIRED WORD, and render void the the teachings of Moses aud the Prophets.

John Whipple Potter Jenks may not have been great, in the sense in which the world counts greatness, but he was a great worker, and the talents with which Nature had endowed him, whether one, five or ten, he improved until they yielded returns an hundred fold. In the annals of his Alma Mater he must always appear as a true benefactor, providentially raised up for the work which he was permitted to accomplish. As the years go by the alumni will gaze with renewed interest upon his portrait, placed by his loving children in the midst of the labors of his hands, recognizing it as the portrait of one who devoted his energies and strength to the founding of a Museum which bears his name, and thus gave facilities for instruction in one of the noblest and most interesting of all studies, that of Natural History.

www.ingramcontent.com/pod-product-compliance
Lightning Source LLC
Chambersburg PA
CBHW030911260626
47169CB00008B/2799